What Do You Call . . .

✦

. . . the fastest dinosaur in the Olympics? A Prontosaurus.

. . . a cave person who sticks his right arm down an Elasmosaurus's throat? Lefty.

. . . a dinosaur that never gives up? A Try-Try-Tryceratops.

. . . a dinosaur that smashes everything in its path? A Tyrannosaurus Wrecks.

. . . a dinosaur that hangs out between buildings? An Alleysaurus.

DINO-MITE DINOSAUR JOKES

Jeff Rovin

A MINSTREL® BOOK

PUBLISHED BY POCKET BOOKS

New York London Toronto Sydney Tokyo Singapore

This book is a work of fiction. Names, characters, places, and incidents either are products of the author's imagination or are used fictitiously. Any resemblance to actual events or locales or persons, living or dead, is entirely coincidental.

A MINSTREL PAPERBACK *ORIGINAL*

A Minstrel Book published by
POCKET BOOKS, a division of Simon & Schuster Inc.
1230 Avenue of the Americas, New York, NY 10020

Copyright © 1994 by Jeff Rovin

All rights reserved, including the right to reproduce
this book or portions thereof in any form whatsoever.
For information address Pocket Books, 1230 Avenue
of the Americas, New York, NY 10020

ISBN: 0-671-88258-9

First Minstrel Book printing June 1994

10 9 8 7 6 5 4 3 2

A MINSTREL BOOK and colophon are registered trademarks of
Simon & Schuster Inc.

Cover art by Gary Johnson

Printed in the U.S.A.

Introduction

✦

Here's a question we'll bet you can answer: How can you find out more about the Age of the Dinosaurs?

Easy. Go to their birthday party.

Though the last of the dinosaurs died about sixty-five million years ago, we've brought them back to life, along with cave dwellers and prehistoric mammals (who did *not* live in the Age of Dinosaurs), in this collection of jokes, riddles, puns, and knock-knocks.

As a matter of fact, we have a theory: We think it was the evolution of humor that caused the dinosaurs to become extinct. When they realized how much fun it was to laugh, the dinosaurs just went pulling one another's legs for years and years . . . and now they're all snakes!

Will these jokes make you smilodon? You bet! (A smilodon is a prehistoric cat about the size of a tiger, and we're not lion! In fact, all of the prehistoric animals mentioned in this book are real.)

✦

Q: What did the baby Apatosaurus get when the papa Apatosaurus sneezed?

A: Out of the way.

"I hated playing hide-and-seek with Apato!" a prehistoric animal said to her dad.

"Why?"

"Because his neck is so long that wherever we hid, Apato saw us."

✦

Peter Pteranodon folded his wings and said to his dad, "I hate racing sister Dinah back to the nest. I *never* win."

"Cheer up," said Papa Pteranodon. "Nobody likes a saur loser."

Actually, Peter's sister was so fast that when she sped by, other Pteranodons used to shout, "Wow! Look at that Dinah Soar!"

✦

Q: What did the Stegosaurus say when a Triceratops backed into him?
A: "I get the point!"

✦

Q: What do you call a dinosaur who wades in mud?
A: A brown toe saurus.

✦

The saber-toothed tiger arrived at a cave where her friends had been partying with a bunch of cavepeople.

"I see I'm too late," said the tiger.

"Yup," said another. "Everyone's eaten."

"You know," a paleontologist said to her friend, "I love my job because I get to listen to music."

"What kind?" said her friend.

"I get to dig rock."

✦

Q: What do you call a sixty-five-million-year-old dinosaur?

A: A fossil.

Dinosaur Limericks

✦

There once was a dinosaur fellow
Whose skin was a cowardly yellow.
"It used to," he said, "be a bright red,
Until I heard T rex's bellow!"

A dinosaur said to his buddy,
"I do not want to bathe in the sea."
First his pal blinked, then said, "But you stink!"
"Better that than ex-stinct, you'll agree."

Sydney Studies Dinosaurs

◆

The teacher said, "Sydney, what kind of animal was the fierce Allosaurus?"

Sydney thought for a moment, then replied, "An endangering species?"

Unhappy with that answer, the teacher asked another question.

"What would we need, Sydney, if we found an Allosaurus alive today?"

The little girl thought long and hard and said, "About sixty-five million candles?"

Frustrated beyond belief, the teacher said, "Sydney, the Allosaurus was a dinosaur. Now, can you tell me what this swift, giant creature ate?"

Sydney thought for another moment, then answered, "Anything it wanted?"

Before giving up, the teacher decided to ask Sydney one final question.

"My dear," said the teacher, "can you tell me which dinosaurs had horns?"

"Sure!" said Sydney confidently. "The ones in the orchestra."

But then Sydney surprised the teacher by saying, "Guess what? I know something dinosaurs had that no other animals had."

"What?" asked the teacher.

Sydney smiled. "Baby dinosaurs."

As the teacher was leaving the room, Sydney shouted, "And I know which side the Stegosaurus had its spikes on!"

"Which side?" the teacher asked.

"The outside!"

◆

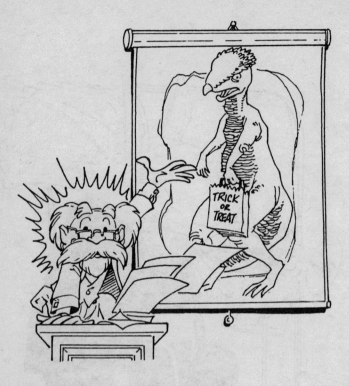

The paleontology professor said to his students, "The bad news about being a Pachycephalosaurus is that they had ugly, bony lumps all over their head. The good news is, they didn't have to dress up for Halloween."

✦

Q: What do you call prehistoric royalty?
A: Princess Di-nosaur.

✦

Then there was the Diplodocus that trampled Di's husband and made messy foot prince . . .

✦

Cavewoman Niggins said to cavewoman Noggins, "Say, I hear Nuggins has a necklace made of saber-toothed tiger teeth. How did she get it?"

"Easy," said Noggins. "She was too slow getting her head out of the way."

✦

Q: What was the scariest dinosaur of them all?
A: The Terrordactyl.

✦

The Allosaurus took his seat in the airplane.

"Would you like to see a menu?" asked the flight attendant.

"No," said the dinosaur. "I'd like to see the passenger list."

✦

Then there was the prehistoric animal that never smiled. No joke! Paleontologists have named it the Alloserious.

✦

Then there was the Irishman who was proud that so many dinosaurs came from the Emerald Isle, like Bront O'Saurus, Tyrann O'Saurus, Steg O'Saurus, Ichthy O'Saurus . . .

Q: What does a tyrannosaurus do before it goes to sleep?
A: Preys.

◆

An Apatosaurus went to see a psychiatrist.
"What's your problem?" asked the doctor.

"I'm terrified of tyrannosauruses! Everywhere I look, I think I see their awful, hooked hands reaching out for me! Can you help me?"

"No problem," said the psychiatrist. "I'm used to treating claws-trophobia."

✦

Q: What's worse than a Brontosaurus with a sore throat?
A: A saber-toothed tiger with a toothache.

✦

Q: Why are dinosaurs such bad storytellers?
A: Because their tails go on much too long.

✦

Q: And do you know what kind of tales dinosaurs told?
A: Prehi-stories.

✦

"Did you hear?" one scientist said to another. "I've successfully bred a parrot and a Pterodactyl!"

"Really?" said the other scientist. "And what did you get?"

"I'm not sure, but when it talks, everyone listens!"

✦

13

The curator of the dinosaur museum told the board of directors, "The good thing is, the budget cuts won't affect us. We're already down to a skeleton crew."

Then there was the Allosaurus that always made snap judgments . . .

✦

. . . and the Apatosaurus who decided that the only thing worse than being chased by a meateater is being chased by two meateaters.

✦

Q: What do paleontology students do before a test?
A: Bone up.

Q: What do you call the gooey stuff between dinosaurs' toes?

A: Slow cavepeople.

What do you call a time of . . .

✦

. . . prehistoric pigs? Jurassic Pork.

. . . feminist dinosaurs? The Ms. Ozoic Era.

. . . polite cavepeople? The Please-tocine Epoch.

. . . unhealthy dinosaurs? The Trias-sick Period.

✦

Then there was the Mamenchisaurus who tripped in his vegetable garden and ended up with a yard full of squash.

✦

Q: What did cavepeople put on their food to make it tastier?
A: Dino-sauce.

✦

"Did you hear?" Mrs. Allosaurus said to her husband. "A herd of Triceratops has moved into the neighborhood."

"That's wonderful," said Mr. Allosaurus. "Let's have them for dinner."

Daffy Dinosaur Definitions

✦

Dimetrodon: What the dimet did when the traffic light changed.

Iguanadon: Extra hardware for an iguan's computer.

Archaeopteryx: What an archeop does in the circus.

Triceratops: What triceras like to spin.

Saltopus: What you do when the cat has no taste.

✦

Q: Where does a Diplodocus wipe its feet?

A: On a diplomat.

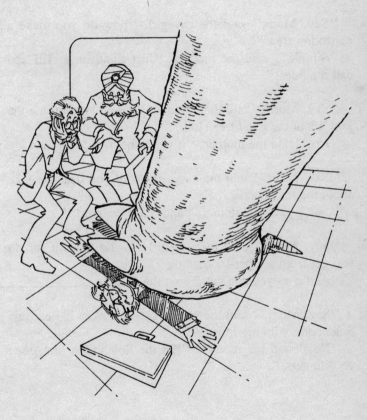

Say, Mom . . .

✦

"Say, Mom," said the cavegirl, "how do you make a mastodon stew?"

"Simple," said the mother. "Just stand on a cliff and call it names."

"Say, Mom," said the cavegirl, "would you tell me the joke about the giant tree sloth?"

"No," said the mother, "it would be over your head."

"Say, Mom," said the cavegirl, "did you hear the joke about the Ice Age?"

"Yes," said the mother, "and it left me cold."

"Say, Mom," said the cavegirl, "what kind of fur do you get from a saber-toothed tiger?"

"As fur as you can get," said the mother.

"Say, Mom," said the cavegirl, "is it okay if I eat this Solenodon with my fingers?"

"No," said the mother. "Eat the Solenodon first, *then* your fingers."

For Scholars Only

✦

Are you up on your science? Do you know your history? Your literature? If so, try these on your funny bone.

Q: What is Henry Wadsworth Longfellow's famous poem about a seafaring tyrannosaur?

A: "The Rex of the Hesperus."

Q: What do dinosaurs exhale?

A: Carboniferous dioxide.

Q: What kind of dinosaur did Sir Richard F. Burton seek in Africa?

A: The Saurus of the Nile.

Q: What are the names of the most famous dinosaur authors?

A: The Bronto sisters.

Some Dinosaur Knock-Knocks

✦

Knock, knock.
Who's there?
Ivan.
Ivan who?
Ivan awful pain where an Elasmosaurus bit me!

Knock, knock.
Who's there?
Juan.
Juan who?
Juan Allosaurus can eat a whole Camptosaurus!

Knock, knock.
Who's there?
Tank.
Tank who?
Tank you for not squashing me, Brachiosaurus!

What do you call . . .

✦

. . . a dinosaur that goes ''whoo-whoo!'' Daffy Duckbill.

. . . a dinosaur that smashes everything in its path? A Tyrannosaurus Wrecks.

. . . the most ferocious prehistoric bug of them all? A Tyr*ant*osaurus.

. . . the fastest dinosaur in the Olympics? A Prontosaurus.

. . . a caveperson who sticks his right arm down an Elasmosaurus's throat? Lefty.

. . . a dinosaur that never gives up? A Try-Try-Tryceratops.

. . . a dinosaur that hangs out between buildings? An Alleysaurus.

. . . a dinosaur that tilts at windmills? A Pteranodon Quixote.

. . . a prehistoric woodcutter? A Dinosaw.

✦

Q: What are two things a dinosaur can't have for dinner?
A: Breakfast and lunch.

✦

One Diplodocus said to the other, "What's the fastest way for me to get a quick snack?"

The other Diplodocus looked up from the tree it was eating. "Easy. Take the shortest route."

And what do you call a Stegosaurus . . .

✦

. . . with no meat on its bones? A Stickosaurus.

. . . who's caught in quicksand? A Stuckosaurus.

. . . who works with plaster? A Stuccosaurus.

. . . who plays with blocks? A Stackosaurus.

Q: What kind of dinosaur has no wings but flies all over?
A: One that doesn't bathe.

"Michael Bud," said the teacher, "would you please spell Stegosaurus for the class?"

"Sure," said Michael. "S-T-E-G-0."

"Right so far. But what's at the end?"

Michael said, "A spiked tail."

◆

Q: What did it cost the Apatosaurus when the meateater bit off its nose?
A: A scent.

Ollie Ornithopsis and Dickie Diceratops

✦

Ollie Ornithopsis asked Dickie Diceratops, "Do you know how to make a dinosaur shake?"

"Sure," said Dickie. "Sneak up behind it and roar like an Allosaurus!"

Ollie asked Dickie, "And do you know how to make a Camptosaurus float?"

"Sure," said Dickie. "Drop it in the ocean."

Later, Ollie asked Dickie, "Do you know the best way to talk to an Allosaurus?"

"Sure," said Dickie. "Long distance."

Much later, Ollie asked Dickie, "Do you know the best way to prevent wounds caused by biting dinosaurs?"

"Sure," said Dickie. "Don't bite any."

Still later, Ollie asked Dickie, "Do you know what would happen if a Red-Billed Rebachisaurus fell in the Blue Danube?"

"Sure," said Dickie. "It'd get wet."

Finally, Ollie asked Dickie, "What looks just like half a Megalosaurus?"

Dickie replied, "The other half."

✦

Q: What did the field of grapes say when the herd of Apatosaurs walked through them?

A: Nothing. They just let out a little wine.

One saber-toothed tiger said to the other, "I hear you're becoming a vegetarian."

"That's right. I'm only eating beans from now on."

"Oh? What kind?"

The saber tooth replied with a grin, "Human."

✦

Mrs. Cosey asked the class, "Can anyone tell me how the dog-sized pony, the eohippus, evolved?"

Little Sheena raised her hand. "I can! It just whinnied and whinnied until it became hoarse."

✦

Q: What did the cavewoman say when a lemon tree fell on her pet saber-toothed tiger?

A: Nothing. She just stood there with a sour puss.

✦

Cavewoman Gletzl asked caveman Uth, "Have you ever hunted bear?"

"No," Uth replied. "I usually wear a loincloth."

✦

Q: What's a dinosaur's favorite playground attraction?
A: The see-saurus.

What's the difference between . . .

✦

. . . a Brontosaurus caught by a Tyrannosaurus and a lollipop. None! They both get licked!

. . . a thunderstorm and a dinosaur who's been nipped by a meateater? One pours rain, the other roars pain.

. . . a mastodon at La Brea and an apprentice weaver? One's caught among tar pits, the other's taught among carpets.

Alphabet Evolution

♦

How do you make dinosaurs sleepy?
Add an *n* and they become "dinosnores."

How do dinosaurs shop?
They add a *t* and turn into "dinostores."

How do dinosaurs win hockey games?
They add a *c* and *r* and become "dinoscorers."

How do dinosaurs make their favorite dessert?
They add an *m* and make "dinos'mores."

✦

Q: What song did the paleontologist sing when she entered the petrified forest?
A: "Wooden It Be Nice?"

✦

Then there was the dinosaur who attributed his weight gain to "heavylution" . . .

✦

Q: What do you call a bird after a Tyrannosaurus bites it?
A: Shredded tweet.

✦

Then there was the Tyrannosaurus who described the Apatosaurus herd as a perfect meating place . . .

✦

. . . and the caveperson who sat awake all night, wondering where the sun went, until it suddenly dawned on him . . .

✦

. . . and the dinosaur who couldn't fall asleep, so she lay on the edge of the cliff and eventually fell off.

✦

Q: What did the Chasmosaurus break when it roared?
A: The silence.

✦

Q: What did prehistoric canaries say?
A: *CHEEP!!! CHEEEEEEEPP!!!*

Gregory Studies Dinosaurs

✦

"Class," said the science teacher, "can anyone tell me what made the Ornitholestes fast?"

"Sure," said Gregory. "When it couldn't catch anything to eat."

"Class," said the science teacher, "can anyone tell me why the Tyrannosaurus rex had a short neck and big head and walked on two legs?"

"I can," said Gregory. "Because if it had a long neck and small head and walked on four legs, it would be an Apatosaurus."

"Class," said the science teacher, "what is meant by 'the Great Dinosaur Extinction'?"

Gregory raised his hand. "It's when the dinosaurs went in one era and out the other."

"Class," said the science teacher, "who can tell me which prehistoric animal had the best vision?"

"I can," said Gregory. "The woolly mammoth did."

"And how do you know that?"

" 'Cause it lived in the Eyes Age."

"Class," said the science teacher, "when the continents were all together, they were called Pangaea. Who can tell me what we called them when they flew apart?"

Gregory raised his hand and shouted, "Peter Pangaea!"

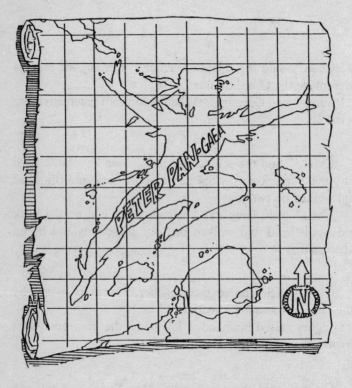

"Class," said the science teacher, "according to current theory, when did the Archaeopteryx, the earliest kind of bird, evolve?"

Gregory raised his hand. "On a Flyday?"

"Class," said the science teacher, "who can tell me what was smaller than a Stegosaurus's very little mouth?"

Gregory raised his hand. "What the Stegosaurus ate."

"Class," said the science teacher, "which dinosaur had its eyes closest together?"

Gregory raised his hand. "The smallest one."

◆

Cavewoman Rubb said to cavewoman Ecka, "I wonder why those mastodons are walking around the lake instead of through it."

"Maybe they're not wearing their swimming trucks."

Q: When are dinosaurs too gross?
A: When there are 288 of them.

✦

Q: Why didn't the Allosaurus cross the road?
A: Because it wasn't chicken.

✦

Q: What did the dinosaur get when it ran through a field of four-leaf clovers?
A: A rash of good luck.

What do you get if you cross . . .

◆

. . . a computer and a Tyrannosaurus rex? A computer with a vicious byte.

. . . a grasshopper and a dinosaur? Gigantic holes in your yard.

. . . a fly with a Pteranodon? I don't know, but forget about the fly paper!

. . . explosives with a prehistoric animal? Dino-mite.

. . . a dinosaur and salted cabbage? Dinosauerkraut.

. . . a comedian and a Tyrannosaurus? Someone with a biting sense of humor.

✦

Q: What do you call a Tyrannosaurus rex comedian?
A: Prehysterical.

✦

"Did you hear?" Wanda Walgettosuchus said to Vicki Vectisaurus. "Tommy Trachodon was struck in the mouth by lightning!"
"Really! What happened?"
"He got the first electric bill in history!"

✦

Q: What does a girl dinosaur call a boy dinosaur with three horns on his head, a beak, lumpy green skin, and big feet?

A: Cute.

Caveman Woog said to caveman Oog, "I have good news and bad news. The good news is, our friend Shmoog killed a saber-toothed tiger all by himself."

"That's great! What's the bad news?

"The bad news is, the tiger choked while eating Shmoog."

✦

Later, caveman Woog said to caveman Oog, "I have good news and bad news. The bad news is, our friend Gnoog had his left side chewed to bits by a smilodon!"

"That's terrible! What's the good news?"

"The good news is, Gnoog is all right."

✦

Q: What do you use to take an Allosaurus's temperature?
A: A thermomeateater.

✦

Q: What kind of prehistoric animal likes to eat out?
A: A dinersaur.

✦

"Say," little Ashley asked Sam, "which do you think would eat more, an elephant or a dinosaur?"

"An elephant," said Sam.

"Why?"

"Because," said Sam, "the dinosaurs are all dead."

The teacher pointed to a map and asked the class, "And where was the largest dinosaur herd?"

Leslie answered, "In the largest concert hall?"

Q: Where can you find cat fossils?
A: In a mew-seum.

◆

Q: Where do dinosaurs look up synonyms?
A: In the saurus thesaurus.

◆

Q: Why did the Struthiomimus raise one leg when it ate?
A: If it raised both legs, it would fall down!

After wandering in northern Montana for a week without spotting a single fossil, the paleontologist turned to his guide with disgust.

"I thought you said you're the best fossil guide in the United States!"

"I am," said the guide. "But we wandered into Canada six days ago."

✦

"Who can spell *Pteranodon* for me?" the teacher asked the class.

Rufus rose and said, "T-E-R-A-N-O-D-O-N."

"Ah," the teacher said, "but where's the *P?*"

Rufus said, "I had it for dinner last night."

✦

Q: What is a plant-eating dinosaur's favorite beverage?
A: Root beer.

✦

"Class," said the teacher, "who can use the word *mister* in a sentence?"

Sammy raised his hand. "The saber-toothed tiger tried to catch the cavewoman, but he missed her."

Q: What did the Triceratops wear on its legs?
A: Tricerabottoms.

"Class," said the teacher, "what was the biggest dinosaur that ever lived?"

Gregory asked, "You mean tallest, widest, or longest?"

"Tallest."

"Carnivore or herbivore?"

"Herbivore."

"Bird-hipped or reptile-hipped?"

"It doesn't matter!"

"Jurassic or Cretaceous?"

"Whatever!"

"Biped or quadruped?"

"QUADRUPED!"

Gregory thought for a moment. "I have no idea."

◆

Some Books About Prehistoric Animals

✦

The Ice Age by I. M. Freezin

More About the Ice Age by I. C. Lands

Chased by a Tyrannosaurus by Auda DeWay

The Hungry Dinosaur by M. T. Beli

Among the Cave Dwellers by Ima Ney and R. Thal

Volcanic Eruptions by Ed S. Hott

Assembling Dinosaur Skeletons by Ms. Inga Peese

How Did the Dinosaurs Die? by Maas X. Tinction

Cooking Mastodons by ''Big'' Stu Potts

The Origin of the Tar Pits by Wyatt Bubbles

How Many Dinosaurs Were There? by Lots N. Lotts

How Powerful Were Dinosaurs? by Vera Strong

Dinosaur Footprints by Marx N. D. Mudd

How to Dig Fossils by Neil Down

A Visit to the Museum by C. D. Bones

Another Visit to the Museum by Seymour Bones

Fossilized Eggs by M. T. Shells

All About Saber-Toothed Tigers by Nast E. Katz

All About Cavepeople by Earl E. Mann

Did a Comet Kill the Dinosaurs? by May B. Sew
I Fought a Saber-Tooth Tiger and Lived! by Claude Badly

A Visit to the Museum
by C.D. BONES

Q: What's the difference between someone telling a president to get down and someone who spots a Corythosaurus?

A: One yells, ''Duck, Bill Clinton!'' and the other yells, ''Duckbill dinosaur!''

Then there was the mama Stegosaurus who ate silverware so her babies would be born with plates and forks . . .

✦

. . . and the mama Ichthyosaurus who ate a piano so her babies would have musical scales.

✦

Q: If a mastodon's head is pointing east, which way is its tail pointing?

A: Down.

✦

Q: Why does a Brachiosaurus have such a long neck?

A: Because its head is so far from its body.

✦

Q: How far could an Allosaurus chase its prey into a hot desert?

A: Halfway. After that, it's chasing its prey *out* of the hot desert.

✦

Q: Could a Stegosaurus jump higher than a mountain?

A: It sure could! Mountains can't jump.

✦

Then there was the Elasmosaurus who swam through the ocean, snapping down shellfish until it became mussel-bound . . .

✦

Needing a new loincloth, caveman Gloob attacked a saber-toothed tiger. Though he was able to poke out its eye, the tiger got away.

Setting out in pursuit, Gloob met caveman Glib, who was coming the other way. "I'm looking for a saber-toothed tiger with one eye," said Gloob.

Glib said, "Wouldn't you have better luck using them both?"

Silly Dinosaur Riddles

✦

Q: Why wasn't the Styracosaurus able to sleep for days?
A: Because it slept nights.

Q: After surviving several harsh Ice Age winters, what did the three-year-old mastodon become?
A: Four.

Q: How many dinosaurs lived on vegetables?
A: None. They all lived on the earth.

Q: What kind of Brachiosaurus was not above six feet?
A: One that was lying on its side.

Q: And what kind of Brachiosaurus was born without teeth?
A: All of them.

Q: How could a herd of Apatosaurs standing at the base of a volcano survive unharmed?
A: It wasn't erupting.

Q: What dinosaur had the largest nose?

A: Tyranno de Bergerac.

During a fossil dig in the Gobi Desert, assistant paleontologist Melanie Berger came running into the tent of the scientist in charge of the expedition.

"Dr. Blyth!" she yelled. "I'd like to report that we have found a dinosaur alive underground!"

"You're kidding!!"

"Yes," she said, "but I'd *like* to report it."

◆

Q: Did dinosaurs have a king and queen?

A: They sure did! You can tell by the foot prince they left behind.

More what's the difference between . . .

✦

. . . cracks in a baseball bat and a prehistoric forest? One has wood dents, the other dense woods.

. . . a Stegosaurus and a neat mail carrier? One has a mighty tail, the other tidy mail.

. . . an eager canary and woolly mammoths? One's an early bird, the other a burly herd.

. . . a coyote and a saber-toothed tiger? One's a prairie howler, the other a hairy prowler.

. . . an itchy dog and a Triceratops being chased by a predator? One's got ticks and fleas, the other just flees.

✦

Q: What was the biggest prehistoric bug of them all?
A: The mam-moth. It was even bigger than the gi-ant!

Advice From Dr. Colón, Dinosaur Veterinarian

◆

"Doctor, what do you give a seasick dinosaur?"
"Plenty of room."

"How much do you charge a dinosaur for an office visit?"
"Two thousand dollars."
"Why so much?"
"Fifty for the visit, the rest for a new table."

"What do you do for a wounded Pteranodon?"
"Bring it to the hospital."
"Why?"
"They have a new wing there."

✦

Q: What kind of dinosaur is big and yucky?
A: A Stegosewer.

✦

Q: What did dinosaurs get on their birthdays?
A: A year older.

✦

Then there was the dinosaur that went to sleep in a pool of petroleum so it could wake up oily in the morning.

✦

Q: What did dinosaurs do when it rained?
A: Got wet.

✦

Q: What dinosaur was green and brown and could see equally as well from either end?

A: A Triceratops with its eyes shut.

Q: What did the Apatosaurus and Stegosaurus have in common?

A: "Osaurus."

Elizabeth and Heather, Paleontologists

✦

Elizabeth asked Heather, "Where can you find fossilized cats, dogs, and goldfish?"

"In a petrified forest."

Elizabeth frowned. "Very funny. And where can you find a petrified forest?"

"Oh, they've got branches everywhere."

"It's interesting," said Elizabeth as she studied the fossil in her laboratory. "This skeleton appears to have come from North America."

"What part?" asked Heather.

"All of it," Elizabeth replied.

✦

Q: What do you call a singing dinosaur bone?
A: A do-re-mi-fa-sol. *(Run the last two words together.)*

✦

Q: What are a baby dinosaur's favorite toys?
A: Tricera-tops.

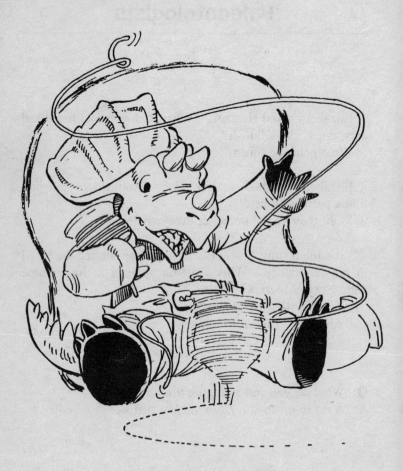

Linda Studies Dinosaurs

✦

"Today," said the teacher, "our lesson will be on the dinosaur."

Linda looked around. "Do you think we'll all fit?"

"Linda," said the teacher, "let's see what you know. Spell *Tyrannosaurus*.

Linda said, "T-I-R-A-N-N-I—"

"Excuse me," said the teacher, "but *Tyrannosaurus* has no *i*'s."

Linda asked, "Then how does it see?"

"Let's try another question," the teacher said to Linda. "Which animal was the forerunner of the modern-day horse?"

Linda thought for a moment, then answered, "The stegos-horse?"

The teacher gave Linda one more chance.
"What do you call a dinosaur that eats meat?"
Linda said, "Hungry?"

✦

Then there was the Brontosaurus who wrote its autobiography. It was quite a tall tale . . .

✦

. . . and the dinosaur who fell in the fiery volcano and invented barbecue saurus.

Jesse Studies Dinosaurs

✦

"Class," said the teacher, "if a biped was a dinosaur with two legs, and a quadruped was a dinosaur with four legs, which do you think was fastest?"

Jesse answered, "A moped?"

"Class," said the teacher, "if the Ice Age produced the most ice, and the Stone Age produced the most stone tools, which age produced the most clothing?"

Clever Jesse answered, "The Garb Age?"

"Class," said the teacher, "why do you think there are so few books written on seagoing dinosaurs?"

Jesse raised his hand. "Because the ink washes off their skins?"

The teacher was asking the children what their parents did for a living. When she got to Jesse, the boy replied, "My dad is a dinosaur hunter."

"You mean a paleontologist?"

"No. I mean he goes out and hunts dinosaurs."

"But there aren't any more dinosaurs," the teacher said.

Jesse smiled. "See how good my dad is?"

The teacher said, "Jesse, since you know so much about dinosaurs, which one required the least amount of food?"

Jesse answered, "An Apatosaurus."

"But those long-necked beasts were *huge!*"

"I know," said Jesse, "but when they ate, a little went a long way.

Determined to educate Jesse, the teacher asked, "What did prehistoric people draw in the caves at Lascaux?"

Jesse answered, "Breath?"

The teacher pressed ahead. "How long were a Brontosaurus's legs?"

Jesse replied, "Long enough to reach the ground."

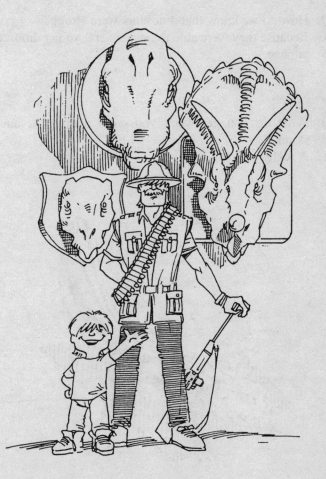

Finally, the poor teacher said, "Jesse, can you name six dinosaurs?"

"Sure," Jesse said. "One Tyrannosaurus rex and five Triceratops."

Q: How do we know that dinosaurs were strong?

A: Because they were able to raise several young dinosaurs at once.

✦

Q: What do you get when you cross a dinosaur and a skunk?

A: A really big stinker.

What kind of prehistoric animals . . .

◆

. . . always sit in rows? Pterodactyls (tier o' dactyls).

. . . live in Iran? Pteranodons (Teheran-odons).

. . . always have spare change? Dimetrodons (Dime-tro-dons).

. . . know how to work computers? Trilobites (trilo-bytes).

Q: Did the ocean-going Ichthyosaurs ever go on dates?

A: Sure! They went out with the tide.

✦

Q: What has a spiked tail, plates on its back, and sixteen wheels?

A: A Stegosaurus on roller skates.

"Say," cavewoman Pegg said to cavewoman Megg, "How many saber-toothed tigers do you think it would take to make a coat?"

"I don't know," said Megg. "I didn't even know they could sew."

Q: What do you get when you cross a Tyrannosaurus and another Tyrannosaurus?

A: Nothing. No one would dare double-cross a Tyrannosaurus!

✦

Then there was the herd of Brachiosaurs who marched single file, even though they hated being necks in line . . .

✦

Q: What do you get when you cross a dog and a dinosaur?

A: I don't know, but its bite would be worse than its bark.

✦

"There I was," Sam told Mike, "far from home with dinosaurs to the left of me, dinosaurs to the right!"

"My goodness! What did you do?"

Sammy said, "I left the museum."

✦

Q: Who was the Lone Ranger's prehistoric sidekick?

A: Bronto.

✦

Then there was the fight with the Triceratops that left the Tyranno sore . . .

✦

Q: Which dinosaur was covered with leaves?
A: The Treeceratops.

A little Archaeopteryx said to its friend, "I just ran over an Ornitholestes!"

"How?"

"Simple. I climbed its tail, scurried down its back, and jumped off its head!"

Fossil Fools

✦

Q: What's the best kind of workers to have when you dig for fossils?
A: A skeleton crew.

✦

Q: How do you get fossils to a museum?
A: By Bonestoga wagon.

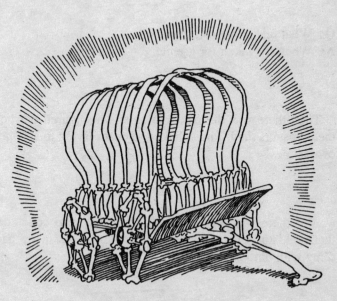

Q: How do you know a dinosaur skeleton doesn't enjoy being in a museum?

A: Because its heart isn't in it.

✦

Q: Do fossil hunters have a good sense of humor?

A: Sure! They're used to taking ribs.

✦

Q: Why are dinosaur fossils so heavy?

A: Because they make a skele-ton!

✦

Q: What makes a fossil grumpy?

A: When it's taken for granite.

✦

Then there was the paleontologist who figured out how the dinosaurs died: They choked to death trying to say their own names!

✦

And there was the other paleontologist who concluded that prehistoric beasts stayed afloat on the ocean by paddling with dino's oars . . .

✦

Q: What do paleontologists shout when they find a pair of dinosaur leg bones?

A: Hip, hip, hooray!

Q: Why were mammals cooler than dinosaurs during the summer?

A: Because they were hair-conditioned.

Q: If twin Apatosaurs wander away at birth, one to the North Pole and the other to the South Pole, will they still grow up to be the same?

A: No! There'll be a world of difference between them.

✦

Q: Why were Apatosaurs such bad dancers?

A: Because they had two left feet.

✦

Q: What's the difference between a school degree and a Diplodocus's mother?

A: Nothing! Both are diplomas.

✦

Preparing his young ones for life on their own, the papa Stegosaurus said, "What steps would you take if a Tyrannosaurus rex suddenly charged?"

A little Stegosaurus piped up, "Great big ones."

✦

The Triceratops said to his mate, "Some dinosaurs think I'm mighty, others think I'm weak. What do you think?"

She said, "I think you're both."

"Both?"

"Sure," she said. "Mighty weak."

✦

Q: What's the best way to escape an Allosaurus?

A: Alive!

✦

Then there was the Centrosaurus who became the toast of the Cretaceous when he didn't get out of the way of the erupting volcano . . .

✦

Q: What did the Allosaurus say to its prey?
A: "It's been nice gnawing you!"

✦

Q: Why didn't the Allosaurus like the Stegosaurus?
A: She just couldn't stomach him.

✦

Q: What's the difference between Mr. Spock and Captain Kirk and a pair of famous dinosaurs?
A: The first are *Star Trek*'s, the second are *T. rex* stars.

✦

Jack and Jill went up the hill
To fetch a pail of water.
At the peak, they heard a shriek
And saw a herd of duckbills.
"Boy," Jack said to Jill, "are *we* in the wrong nursery rhyme!"

✦

After reading a book about photo safaris into the jungle, a little girl asked her father, "Dad, are there such things as dinosaur safaris?"

"Not safaris I know."

✦

As she left the fossil site for the day, the paleontologist entered everything she'd found in the log.

"Dominick," she called to her researcher as he was leaving, "have all your fossils been checked?"

"No," he said. "Off white."

Q: Which dinosaur swung through the trees on vines?
A: The Tarzankylosaurus.

Q: What are the favorite breakfast cereal of Tyrannosaurs?
A: *Trice*ratops Krispies.

◆

Then there was the dumb fossil hunter who got fired for throwing the broken ones away . . .

. . . and the growing Brontosaurus who couldn't stand his neck any longer.

✦

"Cindy," said the fifth-grade teacher, "I'll give you extra credit if you can tell me something a paleontologist might say about a fossil."

· The girl scratched her head and said, "Boy, this is sure hard!"

"Correct!" the teacher said.

✦

Q: What's the difference between dinosaurs and the letter *q* in "quiet"?

A: Nothing. Both were there before *u* and *i*.

✦

The paleontology professor asked her class, "Where would you have found dinosaur snails?"

A student replied, "At the end of dinosaurs' fingers!"

✦

Q: What did the caveman say when his tribe ran off and left him surrounded by saber-toothed tigers?

A: "Fangs alot!"

✦

"Class," said the teacher, "what did dinosaurs eat?"
Little Rita replied, "A few of them ate automobiles."
"Automobiles? But they weren't invented yet."
Rita pouted. "Then why did you tell us that some dinosaurs were carnivorous?"

Q: What's the difference between children playing a famil-
iar game and cavepeople hunting for fur?

A: The first are hide 'n' seeking, the second are seekin'
hide.

✦

Megan said to Monica, "Did you hear about the Tyrannosaurus who accidentally clawed another, and soon the
whole herd was brawling?"

"I see," said Monica. "The fight started from scratch."

✦

The teacher said to his class, "Many of the ornithischian,
or bird-hipped, dinosaurs were very fast. Do you think they
were very smart?"

Cliff raised his hand. "Not if they were also bird-
brained."

✦

Then there was the aspiring fossil assembler who had to
bone up for her exams . . .

✦

. . . and the male Apatosaurus who saw a female Apatosaurus in the middle of the lake and felt she was worth wad-
ing for . . .

✦

A visitor went to the La Brea Tar Pits and saw a smilodon fang suddenly come bubbling to the top of one of the black pools. When she thought that no one was looking, she grabbed the fang and hid it in her bag.

But a security officer saw her and came over.

"You're not allowed to remove fossils from the park," he said, taking the fang from her. "Is this all you have?"

"Yes," she said glumly.

"You sure?"

"*Yes,*" she repeated. "That's the tooth, the whole tooth, and nothing but the tooth, so help me, guard."

. . . and the paleontologists who swapped dinosaur fossils for study, feeling that one good Pteranodon deserves another.

✦

Q: What kind of dinosaurs lived in little tins?
A: Saurdines.

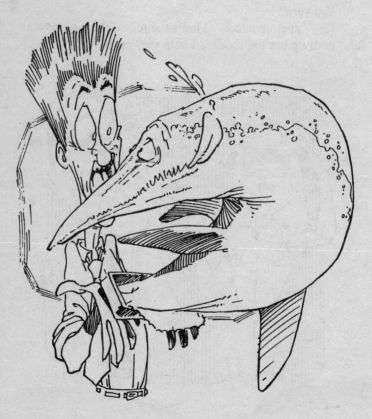

Q: What do you tell paleontologists before they go out fossil hunting?

A: *"Bone appetit!"*

87

About the Author and Illustrator

JEFF ROVIN is the author of more than eighty books, including the bestselling *How to Win at Nintendo Games* series. He has written twelve joke books for kids and adults. He lives in rural Connecticut with his family.

MIKE CHEN has worked with top comic book publishers on such series as *Captain Planet and the Planeteers, M.A.S.K., Archie, The Flash, Starblazers,* and *Teenage Mutant Ninja Turtles*. He currently teaches at the Joe Kubert School of Cartoon and Graphic Art, Inc. in Dover, New Jersey.